the farm!

Lauren Tobia

They're so

tumbly,

wiggly,

jumbly!

Can YOU
do it, too?

Red boots, green boots,
Swishing through the hay.
Bee and Billy

are excited...

They're on the **FARM** today!

"Look! A fluffy hen!"

shouts Bee.
She follows it
around.

It peck-peck-pecks by Billy's feet,

The crumbly crumbs

on the dusty

ground.

Billy spots a round thing,

Underneath a shed.

Gently, slowly, Bee

lifts it out...

"WOW!

Billy's found an

EGG!"

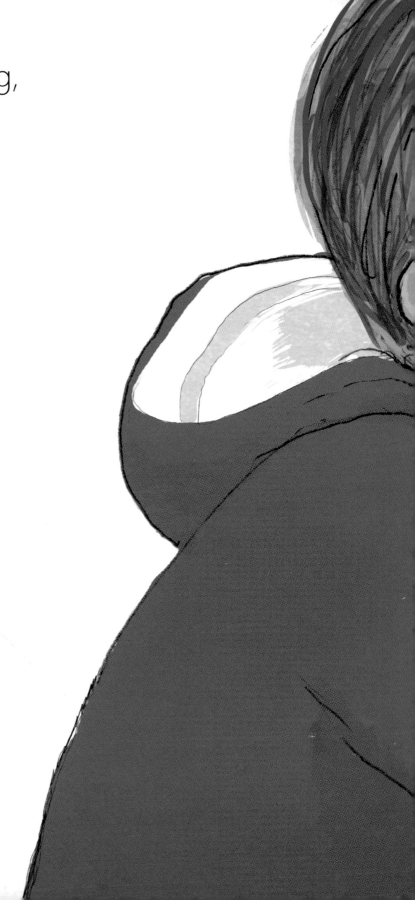

Wriggling piglets in a pen,

How many can you see?

Mummy piggy grunt-grunt-grunts,

Piglets cry, **"Squee s-q-u-e-e!"**

"Now it's time to feed the lambs!"

Bee holds a bottle tight.

But Billy clings onto his Mummy,

"Don't worry. It's all right."

Bee's little lamb is hungry,

It pulls the bottle hard.

Lamb's tail wriggles, Billy giggles,

As Bee chases it round the yard!

Can you spot the guinea pigs?

They're playing hide-and-seek!

Hopping, popping, through the hay,

Chitter-chatter-squeak!

Bee sits down on the scratchy straw,

A soft towel on her knee.

"My guinea pig's called Puzzle.

Stroke her gently, Billy.

See?"

It's noisy in the hen house,
Hens flap and cluck
and scratch.

Billy finds more eggs under a lamp...
Crick! Crack! One's going to hatch!

"Who's inside the barn?" asks Bee.

Calves gaze with gentle eyes.

Wet noses glisten,

long tongues poke out,

LICK!

What a surprise!

Over at the picnic bench,

Mums rummage for a snack.

But Billy isn't hungry,

"Billy! Wait!

Come back!"

"Here I am!" calls Billy.

"I'm bringing in the hay!"

Bee clambers up to help him,

And they play, and play,

and play.

Bee and Billy
   are going home,
Today has been such fun.
They're yawny, sleepy,
   snuggly, tired...

Goodbye,
everyone!